A BEACH FOR THE BIRDS

written and photo-illustrated by

Bruce McMillan

Houghton Mifflin Company Boston 1993

This one is
For the Birds

It is possible to view this barrier beach located in Kennebunk, Maine, without disturbing the Least Terns. The adjacent Wells National Estuarine Research Reserve at Laudholm Farm, P.O. Box 1559, Wells, Maine 04090, and Rachel Carson National Wildlife Refuge, RR2, Box 751, Route 9 East, Wells, Maine 04090 are open to the public. The reserve and refuge have informative visitor centers and nature trails, many wheelchair accessible. They are located off Route 1 and off Route 9, respectively, between Kennebunk and Wells, Maine.

Because this is a barrier beach, winter storms sometimes shift the sands, significantly altering nesting sites from year to year. In 1991 this shift occurred, and there was a loss of nesting area for that season. No chicks were hatched. However, in 1992 the sands shifted again, and nature reversed itself. The nesting area was restored, and the terns came back in greater numbers. Despite naturally occurring changes like these, the greatest habitat threat to the Least Tern continues to be human use and development of the beachfront.

This photographic nature study was conducted during a three-year period from 1989 to 1991. It was done in cooperation with the Maine Audubon Society. Great care was taken to not disturb the birds while photographing them. I know this "beach for the birds" well — I was raised in Kennebunk, Maine, and live in nearby Shapleigh.

Research source assistance was graciously provided by Alfred Mueller, Librarian, Ornithology Library, Peabody Museum, Yale University; and Bradford Blodget, State Ornithologist, Division of Fisheries and Wildlife, Commonwealth of Massachusetts. The text was fact-checked by Jonathan L. Atwood, Manomet Bird Observatory, Manomet, Massachusetts; and Jody Jones, Wildlife Biologist, Maine Audubon Society, Falmouth, Maine.

Photographic Data
Camera: Nikon F4 with MF23 multi-control back
Lenses: Nikkor 24mm AF, 50mm AF, 55mm Micro AF, 85mm AF,
180mm AF, 300mm AF, 500mm reflex, and 600mm ED
Tripod: Bogen 3051 Professional
Film: Kodachrome 64 processed by Kodalux

Designed by Bruce McMillan
Title Text set in Tiffany   Text set in Sabon
Color Separations by Colordot   Printed on Command Satin
Printed and bound by Horowitz/Rae Book Manufacturers, Inc.
Printed in the United States of America
HOR 10 9 8 7 6 5 4 3 2 1

Library of Congress Cataloging-in-Publication Data
McMillan, Bruce.
    A beach for the birds / Bruce McMillan.
        p. cm.
    Summary: Discusses the physical characteristics and habits of the
endangered Least Terns and describes the Maine beach where they spend
the summer and raise their young, parallel to their human neighbors.
    ISBN 0–395–64050–4
    1. Least tern — Maine — Juvenile literature. 2. Seashore ecology —
Maine — Juvenile literature. 3. Beaches — Maine— Juvenile
literature. 4. Endangered species — Maine — Juvenile literature.   [1. Least tern.
2. Sea birds. 3. Seashore ecology. 4. Beaches. 5. Endangered species.]
I. Title.
QL696.C46M35 1993   92–10920
598.3'38 — dc20   CIP
                                             AC

"*While traveling, their light but firm flight is wonderfully sustained, and on hearing and seeing them on such occasions one is tempted to believe them to be the happiest of the happy.*"

—John James Audubon on the Least Tern

Every May, people begin returning to their homes on a coastal Maine beach. Children fly their kites on brisk breezes. This beach lies southeast of the Little River. Across the river another beach lies to the northwest. There are no houses here, but its inhabitants, the Least Terns (*Sterna antillarum antillarum*), arrive on the same kite breezes. Here, the birds will make their summer homes.

The terns have migrated back from their coastal winter homes located somewhere south of the United States and north of Brazil. With an instinctive sense of direction, they have flown here to spend the summer — to nest and to raise their young.

Delicate and graceful with long wingspans and forked tails, they are often called the "swallows of the sea." These smallest of all the terns are one-third the size of common Herring Gulls. Their flight is sometimes light and buoyant. Other times it is dashing and swift, with periods of effortless gliding.

There are only a few undisturbed beaches left for nesting. Because of this scarcity, and because Least Terns were perilously over-hunted for their "fashionable" feathers years ago, their population has declined. In the 1800s they were abundant. Now, Least Terns are an endangered species here and elsewhere. Less than 150 of them summer in Maine, the northernmost range for the Eastern Least Tern. But here on the coast by the Little River, there is still a beach for them.

Like most sea birds, Least Terns don't have brightly colored feathers. Both male and female adults are covered in pure white, slate gray, and crisp black feathers. Their flight feathers are long. Their contour feathers are sleek, evenly spaced, and overlapping. All of the feathers are supported by a lightweight, but strong, framework of hollow bones. With all of these flight-enhancing features, terns don't need camouflage colors to hide them from enemies. They elude danger with their superior flying skills.

In the summer, mature Least Terns are easily distinguished from other types of terns by their distinctive, black-tipped yellow bills. Bird bills are made of a bony core that's covered with keratin — the same substance that people's fingernails are made of. Just as fingernails grow, the Least Tern's bill covering also grows. In the fall, the yellow bill will change color. Black will start growing at the base and slowly spread to the tip until the bill is entirely black. The following spring the bill's yellow color will return gradually, spreading forward from the base of the bill as the black did.

As the terns arrive from their long journey, they gather in a group — a colony. In this colony are twenty to forty birds, loosely dispersed along the beach. They are safer in the colony since there are more eyes to watch for approaching dangers like foxes or dogs.

Many of the terns have been here before. They come back because there are beaches where they can nest, and they can find plenty to eat in the Little River.

The Little River is an abundant food source, so it attracts ocean fish to the mouth of the river. Children cast fishing lines in hopes of catching a three-and-a-half-foot Stripped Bass (*Roccus saxatilis*) or Bluefish (*Pomatomus saltatrix*). Terns fish too, but for much smaller fish. From high above the water they can actually see their prey swimming.

Terns' eyes, like those of most animal hunters, are located toward the front of their head. Inside their eyes are the sight receptors — rods and cones. Terns see in color, as people do, though terns see better. People — and most birds — have an area inside the eye tightly packed with only cones for even more sensitivity — the fovea. Least Terns have not one but two foveas. It's like having a built-in set of binoculars in each eye. It makes them excellent judges of the underwater speed and distance of their prey.

Thirty feet above the water, and with their bills aimed down, the terns search for slender two-to-four-inch fish. When they spot one, they halt their gliding flight. To get a good look they fix their eyes on the fish and hover for about four seconds. Sometimes they hover for up to eight seconds — longer than any other tern. With their eyes still fixed on their prey, they twist their tails and steer themselves into position.

Abruptly, they begin their diving plunge, pulling their wings back to control the speed and depth of their fall. In this streamlined position, they fearlessly streak straight down — headfirst — aimed at the unaware fish. Then — splash — the terns disappear underwater, still on target. Traveling like submerged arrows, they open their bills to catch their prey.

The fish they catch here are usually tiny Sand Lance (*Ammodytes americanus*), sometimes called "sand eels" since they look like miniature eels. Sand Lance swim in schools close to the surface. As they approach and enter the Little River from the ocean, they are pursued by larger fish from below and by terns from above. The fish don't see the flying terns. With white underside feathers, terns blend into the sky and remain hidden.

Least Terns catch their prey underwater, one fish at a time, with open bills. But sometimes the terns are a little off-target. They might still catch a fish by accidentally spearing it on their pointed bill.

When the terns emerge, they are airborne immediately, many times triumphant with a wiggling fish in their bill. Usually, they eat it within seconds, for they can fly and eat at the same time. They use their tongue to guide the fish's head into their throat. Not having any teeth, they swallow it whole. They can't swallow it tail-first because the fish scales would be pointed down their throat, making it difficult or impossible to swallow. When the terns don't choose to eat their catch, they're usually saving it for their mate or one of their chicks.

Like their human neighbors on the other beach, Least Terns require more than food to live. They need water. They get most of their water from an unusual source; it comes from the fish they catch. Sand Lance may swim in salt water, but like all animals, these fish are partly made up of fresh water. So, terns always get "a drink of fresh water" with their meal.

Terns get the rest of the small amount of water they need by doing something people can't do: they drink salt water. Though they can drink fresh water, salt water is more accessible by the ocean. A gland inside the front of their head collects the excess salt from the swallowed water. Then the salt is secreted in concentrated saltwater droplets from nose holes found on the upper bill.

With screams of delight, children splash and jump over the waves on their beach across the river. On the Least Terns' beach, the terns land with a splash, too. They continue to splash as they swim in the calm shallows. Though it looks like play, there's a purpose to their splashing. They are cleaning their feathers. Flight — and in effect life itself — depends on well-maintained feathers. Every day, the terns adjust them, stretching and pulling at those that have become worn out. New ones will grow in during late summer or early fall.

After swimming in the cold ocean, children run to towel themselves dry. They put on shirts to stay warm in the ocean breeze. Terns have their own way of staying warm. They never remove their water-repellent "down jackets" — their feathers. Whether they're swimming, flying or resting, their feathers act as temperature regulators and keep them both dry and warm. Without feathers, the thermal shock of going from cold ocean water to warm air would be too abrupt for the birds' fragile bodies.

On short legs, terns saunter over the sand in a smooth shuffle. Other times they scamper. Either way, their legs alternate back and forth, lifting and stepping. The sand is soft but they don't sink into it. They are light in weight and have webbed feet. As terns' feet flex forward and down, the three "toes" extend out. A fleshy covering unfolds between them like a web. When terns walk on the sand with their broad, flat feet, it's similar to people wearing snowshoes — but terns have "sandshoes."

At this time of year, the breeding season, the "advertising" calls of Least Tern males fill the air. Terns mate every year, starting at age two or three, when they're mature. They bond in male/female pairs, and if all goes well they become parents to a chick or two.

The breeding season starts with aerial courtship dances between the males and females. Then, the females wait on the beach to be fed. The males, flying with fish in their bills, call out, "kidee-kidee . . . kidee-kidee." They can "talk" with their mouths full because bird calls are made in the throat, not the bill. The males land near the females and approach cautiously. By ignoring the males or flying away, the females sometimes reject the fish-carrying males.

Males often circle the females, proudly flicking their bills to show off their prize fish. When a female is receptive to these advances, she lets the male know by crouching down. The male then hops onto the female's back from behind, and the female turns her head. She grasps the gift fish with her bill. Mating takes place and shell-less eggs inside the female are fertilized. The first step has been taken toward creating a new life — a tern chick.

Lifeguards watch out for the safety of everyone on the people's beach, and terns keep watch on theirs. Terns scan their surroundings for approaching danger, and never more than at nesting time.

The female terns settle in an open area above the high tide line and below the dense beach grass. It's a flat, exposed area high on the beach where both males and females can guard against predators. Here, the parents-to-be can take off and land with ease, their wings unobstructed by beach grass. Males stay busy fishing, not only for themselves, but also for their waiting mates. Their mates remain on the beach and select a spot to make their nests.

Children usually build with wet sand by the surf. But terns build higher up, in the dry sand. They make nests called scrapes. The terns, male or female, brace themselves with one foot and, using their other webbed foot like a rake, kick the sand back. These scrapes — barely noticeable depressions in the sand — are nests for their soon-to-be-laid eggs. They usually make many scrapes before the females settle at a nest.

Within the female's body, a thin paste covers and encloses the fertilized eggs, layer by layer, until the shells are thick. Then the females lay their first egg, and two days later, their second. Sometimes they lay only a single egg; other times they may lay three. It seems to depend on how much food is available. The eggs are only an inch-and-a-quarter long, and they're rarely left alone. If a nesting parent must leave to chase away a person or predator, though the eggs are temporarily exposed, their speckled color keeps them hidden.

Natural dangers face the eggs. Storm tides that rise above the normal high water mark can be disasters. Flooding ocean waters can wash away nests and eggs. If this happens early in the season, the adults court and mate again. About three weeks later they're nesting with new eggs. Hopefully it's still early enough in the summer to allow the chicks enough time to grow after hatching.

The eggs need to be protected from intolerable extremes of temperature. On sunny days, the sand gets so hot that barefoot people can't walk on it. On this side of the river, the terns sit on their eggs, protecting them from the hot sunlight with the shade of their own bodies. To keep the eggs cool, the parents-to-be fly down to the ocean, splash about, fly back to their nest, and shake drops of cool ocean water onto the eggs. This offsets the heat of the day. If people approach, the terns are forced to temporarily abandon their eggs, and if the eggs are left exposed too long, they will never hatch. At night the terns continue to sit on their eggs, but now to keep them warm. They blanket their eggs with body warmth from their brood patch.

This small patch of bare skin, the brood patch, appears every year at the start of the breeding season. Both males and females lose a small patch of down feathers on their breast. This skin area thickens with warm blood vessels. As terns prepare to sit on their eggs, they ruffle their breast feathers to fully expose the bare patch. Once the eggs are nestled next to the exposed skin, the adults' body warmth is transferred to them. After nesting is completed, the parents grow back their missing patch of soft, insulating feathers, and the brood patch disappears until next year's breeding season.

During nesting, males continue to bring fish to their mates. But females can and do go fishing themselves. While they fish, the males take over the nesting duties. The fragile eggs are rarely left unattended. Both parents-to-be take turns caring for and incubating their precious eggs.

On the other side of the river, young children and babies are cared for by their parents. Like people, Least Terns are always alert to the needs of their babies — their newborn chicks.

After about twenty-one days of nesting, the eggs have hatched. Tern chicks, like most birds, have pecked their way out from inside the eggs by using a temporary "egg tooth" — a hard calcium deposit found on the end of their beak. Downy-feathered newborn chicks are somewhat hidden in their exposed sand scrape because, like their eggs, they are camouflaged. For the first day or two they stay in their nests, shielded from the hot sun by their parents. Because the empty eggshells might attract predators, the parents pick the shells up in their bills and drop them farther down the beach.

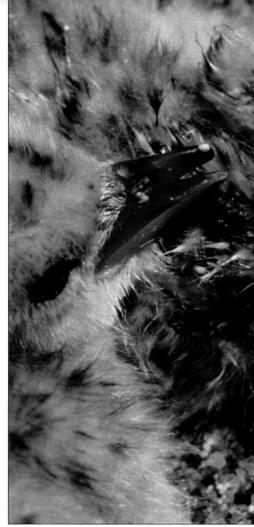

If a predator — like a gull, crow, dog, fox, or person — finds the nesting area, the first tern to spot the approaching danger alerts the rest of the colony with an alarm call. "Zreep . . . zreep . . . zreep!" The terns gather and form an airborne mob. They fearlessly attack, one at a time, even though the trespassers are usually much larger. Terns charge intruding gulls in midair, calling "zreeeeep . . . zreeeeep" until the gulls leave. If the trespasser is on land, the alerted terns dive-bomb the target. At the end of their dive, less than a yard away, they startle the intruder with a loud "zreeeeep" and drop their bomb. As they brake feet-first in the air, they defecate. With excellent aim, they splatter their target.

The "zreep" attack calls are also alarm calls to alert the chicks. When the chicks hear them, they scatter up the beach to the tall grass and hide. They lie flat, completely still. Their beaks blend in with the grass stems. The chicks' backsides stick out, exposed, like human babies who play hide-and-seek but only conceal their heads. Fortunately, the chicks' sandy camouflage keeps them hidden.

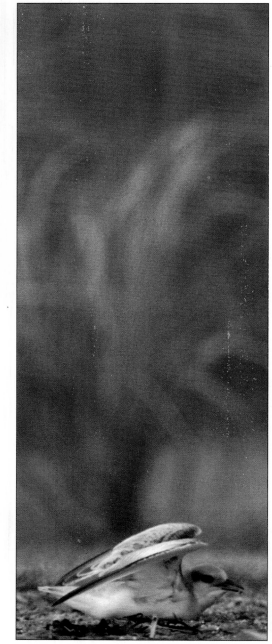

The chicks grow into "runners." Their fluffy down feathers are replaced by new sleek ones; they have the beginnings of flight feathers. Unlike the black and white adult feathers that are yet to grow, the first feathers are still a shade of sandy brown. This protective coloration continues to blend the defenseless terns into their surroundings. But if the young terns spot intruders, they elude them by running in zigzag lines through the dune grass to hide. Now, they hide their whole bodies — not just their heads — among the natural beach debris of seaweed and driftwood.

Though the "runners" often wander away, their parents can always find them by their call. Parents are able to identify their own chicks' "peep . . . peep" after they are only a day old. Two days later, the chicks can pick out their parents' "kip . . . kip" calls. First as chicks, and now as "runners," they rush to greet the calls of their fish-bearing parents. Like their parents, young terns swallow their fish whole, headfirst. Fortunately, parents match the size of their catch to the size of their offspring.

When their feathers are longer and their plumage fuller, young terns discover that something about them has changed. Now three weeks old, they find that their wings have grown enough to take them aloft. They are fledglings. They mimic their parents and take their first short flights. A few days later, they take the next step — they practice diving into the ocean. Fledglings imitate the adults' fishing behavior, but it takes a lot of practice before they're able to catch a fish. Until then, their parents continue to feed them.

Piping Plover (*Charadrius melodus*)

On the far side of the river, children share their beach with friends. On this side, Least Terns have their own "friends" — other birds. One species of bird is their "best friend" — the Piping Plover (*Charadrius melodus*), another endangered species.

Piping Plovers are one of the few species of birds that the terns share the nesting part of the beach with. They eat different aquatic animals: terns eat fish, while plovers eat crustaceans and marine worms. Therefore, they never fight over food. By nesting together, terns protect their own chicks — and plover chicks — by attacking intruders. If this fails, plovers try to distract the intruders by drawing attention to themselves and away from the nesting area. With their Least Tern "friends," Piping Plovers often have a better chance of successfully raising their chicks, though sometimes the colonies attract too many predators.

Red-winged Blackbird (*Agelaius phoenicius*)

Piping Plovers may be one of the few birds allowed in the nesting area, but there are other parts of this beach. There are also other birds to share it.

In the marsh behind, Red-winged Blackbirds (*Agelaius phoenicius*) cling to the dune grass, singing their "kong-ka-ree." Along the edge of the beach, feeding Sanderlings (*Crocethia alba*) run in and out of shallow waves like windup toys.

Common Terns (*Sterna hirundo*), who are almost twice the size of Least Terns, visit the beach to fish. Meanwhile, near the water's edge, Least Terns may calmly sit among a flock of young Bonaparte's Gulls (*Larus ridibundus*), while Herring Gulls (*Larus argentatus*) sit nearby. These Herring Gulls are the same intruders the terns would have chased away from their nesting area, but here they're no threat.

Sanderlings (*Crocethia alba*)

Least Tern lives depend on, and revolve around, two things: food and flight. All summer long they feed and tend to their feathers.

Facing into the breeze, they stand on the tidal part of the beach, balancing comfortably on their short legs. Using their long bills as tools, they preen their feathers. This smoothes and cleans them. Preening isn't done randomly, nor just when the feathers are dirty or out of place. The terns preen regularly. They follow a pattern and pay special attention to certain feathers. They also oil their feathers from a gland at the base of their tail. After rubbing their bill against this gland, they rub the oil onto their feathers. This makes their "down jackets" water-repellent.

At sunset, when children head home to sleep, terns land above the high-tide line on their beach to do the same thing. They settle in for a night of rest, cloaked in darkness.

During the last days of summer, both adult and young terns continue to scratch, stretch, ruffle, oil, sun, bathe, and preen. They must have their feathers in perfect condition for their upcoming journey. The new members of the tern colony, barely two months old and feathered in juvenile plumage, are old enough to migrate. They will be able to fly thousands of miles south to a warm beach for the winter. Here, they will stay for a year or two and mature before returning north as adults.

By late August the sun rises later and sets earlier. Summer is ending. The breeze blows a little cooler. Children start thinking about leaving their vacation homes and going to school. Terns know it's time for them to leave, too. Their fishing season here is just about over.

Instinctively, they know it's time to begin their journey south. They must start their annual migration to another beach where it will be warm during the winter. They must leave behind their summer home, their beach by the Little River. In a few months it will be covered with snow and wrapped in ice.

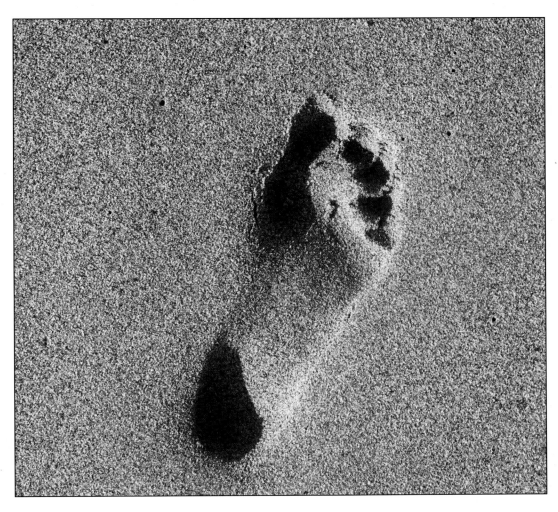

As children head back to their winter homes, Least Terns leave for theirs. The "swallows of the sea" take to the air for their trip south. Footprints left behind in the sand, both terns' and people's, blow away in the ocean breeze or wash away in the incoming tide.

Next year, children will come back to play, and breeding terns will come back to raise another family. Summer after summer, both people and terns will revisit this stretch of sand by the Atlantic Ocean. They'll continue to live side by side as long as there's a beach for the people, as well as a beach for the birds.

LEG BANDS

Lightweight bands are placed on terns' legs by researchers for bird studies and identification. The colored plastic bands are for licensed studies. The plain metal bands are issued by the U.S. Fish and Wildlife Service, and are stamped with a number and address. Anyone who finds the remains of a banded bird should note the location and date. This information and the bands should be sent to the address on the metal band: Bird Banding Laboratory, Office of Migratory Bird Management, Laurel, MD 20708. You'll receive a letter of thanks, and find out where your bird was banded.

Red-winged Blackbird (*Agelaius phoenicius*)

LEAST TERN FACTS

Scientific name: *Sterna antillarum* (*Sterna* means "tern," *antillarum* means "of the Indies").

Preferred common name: Least Tern.

Other common names: Killing Peter, Leastie, Little Kip, Little Striker, Miner Hawk, Striking Peter, Reek, Sand Peter, Sea Swallow, and Silvery Tern.

Subspecies: Eastern Least Tern (*Sterna antillarum antillarum*) breeds along the United States Atlantic and Gulf coasts, with Maine its northernmost range.

Interior Least Tern (*Sterna antillarum athalassos*) breeds along rivers in the Mississippi and Rio Grande river basins.

California Least Tern (*Sterna antillarum browni*) breeds along the California and Mexican coasts.

Related species: Little Tern (*Sterna albifrons*) is slightly larger and has different vocal calls. The Little Tern lives in Africa, Asia, Australia, and Europe.

Range: The Least Tern summers in North America, and winters in Central America and northern South America.

Adult size: The Least Tern is smallest of all the terns, with males — 9″ length, 20″ wingspan, 3.5″ tail, and 1.25″ bill on average — slightly larger than females.

Adult breeding color: Brown eyes, bright yellow bill (usually black-tipped), bright yellow legs and feet, black cap with a white V on the forehead, pale gray back and wings, black line on leading edge of wings, white underside.

Chick color: Brown eyes, brown-black bill, pale pink then orange-brown legs and feet, brown-buff down feathers.

Average age of first breeding: 2–3 years.

Nest: Bare scrape in sand.

Average number of eggs per nest: 2.

Egg size: 1.25″ in length.

Egg color: Light tan with multicolored brown speckles.

Incubation period: 20–22 days.

Food: Small fish that swim close to the surface, such as Sand Lance, as well as herring and silversides; sometimes small shrimp.

Summer/breeding habitat: Sandy beaches, small-pebbled flat expanses, and on rare occasions a flat rooftop; located next to an aquatic food source such as an ocean or river.

Life span: Unknown, though estimated average is 6–7 years, and 21 years has been recorded.

Predators: Cats, coyotes, crows, dogs, foxes, gulls, kestrels, night herons, opossum, raccoons, rats, skunks, and others.

History: Abundant until the 1880s, the Least Tern was hunted nearly to extinction on the United States Atlantic coast. In 1891, as many as 100,000 terns were killed in Virginia to satisfy a fashion trend — tern feathers as decorations on women's hats. In 1913 they became fully protected by the government, and their numbers increased. However, the loss of undisturbed coastal and river habitat to human development kept their numbers from increasing to the nineteenth-century levels. Today, though still a small population, they are able to live successfully alongside people, provided their nests remain undisturbed and their food source unpolluted. In a nine-year period from 1977 to 1986, the total number of breeding pairs recorded on the Atlantic Coast from Maine to Virginia increased by 2,601, from 6,740 in 1977 to 9,341 in 1986.

Species status: The Eastern Least Tern is listed by several states, including Maine, as an endangered species. The mid-Atlantic range of the Eastern Least Tern population appears to be the most stable subspecies population at this time. The California Tern and Interior Least Tern are listed in the United States Endangered Species Act as endangered species.

GLOSSARY

Brood Patch — an area of the breast that is featherless during the breeding season in order to transfer body warmth from nesting parent to egg.

Chick — a newly hatched bird, covered in down feathers.

Colony — a group of certain birds, such as terns, living together.

Color Camouflage — coloration that matches and blends with the surrounding habitat as a means of concealing the animal; sometimes called cryptic coloring.

Contour Feathers — the outermost feathers that form the body outline.

Defecate — to eliminate digestive waste in the form of uric acid and feces.

Down Feathers — the fluffy insulating feathers that cover newborn chicks, and also grow under adult contour feathers.

Egg Tooth — a temporary, hard calcium deposit located on the end of the bill of an about-to-hatch chick; used to peck the shell in a circular line from within so that the end of the shell breaks open like a cap.

Fledgling — a young bird that has grown its first set of flight feathers and is capable of flight.

Flight Feathers — the long, stiff, smooth-surfaced wing and tail feathers necessary for flight.

Fovea — a depression in the eye's visually sensitive retina where only cone receptors, not rods, are densely packed for superior vision; found in both humans and birds; certain birds such as terns have two foveas in each eye (called bifoveal) for even better vision.

Instinct — an inborn drive to perform certain behaviors, such as migration. Birds can perform certain functions automatically, enabling their small brains to function more efficiently.

Keratin — a strong protein substance that forms feathers, fur, hair, and fingernails, as well as the covering of a bird's beak.

Migration — the seasonal journey between two hospitable habitats that are often great distances apart.

Plumage — a bird's feathers.

Predator — an animal that feeds on other animals, such as foxes, who feed on tern chicks, or terns, who feed on small fish.

Preen — to smooth and clean one's feathers, usually with the bill.

Prey — an animal that is the food of other animals, such as tern chicks who are food for gulls and foxes, or small fish who are food for terns.

Scrape — a tern nest which is a barely noticeable depression in the sand; formed by "scraping" the sand with their webbed feet.

Species — a classification for a group of animals who have similar features that distinguish them as a group, and who can breed with other members of their group. For example, the classification for the Least Tern (*Sterna antillarum antillarum*) refers to the genus name —*Sterna*— which is the group name for all types of terns; followed by the species name —*antillarum*— which designates it as a Least Tern; and then the subspecies name —*antillarum*— which in this example happens to be the same name repeated, and designates it as an Eastern Least Tern.

INDEX

SELECTED BIBLIOGRAPHY

Atwood, Jonathan L. and Massey, Barbara W. 1978. Plumages of the Least Tern. *Bird-Banding.* Vol. 49 No. 4: 360–371.

Bent, Arthur Cleveland. 1921. Life Histories of North American Gulls and Terns. *Smithsonian Institution.* Bulletin 113:270–279.

Burger, Joanna. 1987. Physical and Social Determining of Nest-site Selection in Piping Plover in New Jersey. *The Condor.* Vol. 89: 811–818.

Carreker, R.G. 1985. Habitat Suitability Index Models: Least Tern. U.S. Fish and Wildlife Service. *Biological Report 82(10.103).*

Cramp, Stanley, Chief Editor. 1985. *Handbook of the Birds of Europe, the Middle East, and North Africa. The Birds of the Western Palearctic.* Oxford, New York: Oxford University Press.

Dale K. 1976. *Least Tern, Sterna Albifrons, Nesting Habitat in Maine and Its Relevance to the Critical Areas Program.* Maine State Planning Office.

Farner, D.S., King, J.R., and Parkes, K.C. 1973. *Avian Biology,* Vol 3. New York and London: Academic Press, a subsidiary of Harcourt Brace Jovanovich, Publishers.

Farrand, John, Jr. 1983. *The Audubon Society Master Guide to Birding, 2. Gulls to Dippers.* New York: Alfred A. Knopf.

Fisher, James, and Lockley, R.M. 1954. *Sea-Birds, An Introduction to the Natural History of the Sea-Birds of the North Atlantic.* Boston: Houghton Mifflin Company.

Nelson, Bryan. 1980. *Seabirds, Their Biology and Ecology.* London, New York, Sydney, Toronto: The Hamlyn Publishing Group Ltd.

Schreiber, Elizabeth Anne. 1978. *Wonders of Terns.* New York: Dodd, Mead and Company.

Silverman, Marianne. —. *Stewardship Abstract Responsibility: Eastern Heritage Task Force, Sterna antillarum.* The Nature Conservancy. Element Code: ABNKH07090.

Tomkins, Ivan R. 1959. Life History Notes on the Least Tern. *The Wilson Bulletin.* Vol. 71 No. 4: 313–322.